The Two Яichards

The Two Яichards

Vladimir Azarov

EXILE editions

singular fiction, poetry, nonfiction, translation, drama, and graphic books

Library and Archives Canada Cataloguing in Publication

Title: The two Richards / Vladimir Azarov.
Names: Azarov, Vladimir, 1935- author.
Description: Poems. | First letter "R" in "Richard" appears as capitalized Cyrillic
   letter ya on source of information for title.
Identifiers: Canadiana (print) 20210271728 | Canadiana (ebook) 20210271841 |
   ISBN 9781550969450 (softcover) | ISBN 9781550969467 (EPUB) |
   ISBN 9781550969474 (Kindle) | ISBN 9781550969481 (PDF)
Classification: LCC PS8601.Z37 T86 2021 | DDC C811/.6—dc23

Copyright © Vladimir Azarov, 2021
Book designed by Michael Callaghan
Cover painting, *Untitled*, oil on canvas, 1997 © Marc Séguin/SOCAN (2021)
Three illustrations © Kaedán and Kellen Campos-Callaghan
Typeset in Bembo font at Moons of Jupiter Studios
Published by Exile Editions Ltd ~ www.ExileEditions.com
144483 Southgate Road 14—GD, Holstein, Ontario, N0G 2A0
Printed and Bound in Canada by Gauvin

We gratefully acknowledge the Canada Council for the Arts,
the Government of Canada, the Ontario Arts Council, and
Ontario Creates for their support toward our publishing activities.

Canadian sales representation: The Canadian Manda Group,
664 Annette Street, Toronto ON M6S 2C8.
mandagroup.com 416 516 0911

North American and international distribution, and U.S. sales:
Independent Publishers Group, 814 North Franklin Street,
Chicago IL 60610. ipgbook.com 1 800 888 4741

WHAT IS IT NOW AND THEN?

A Chekhovian Prelude

*"For Christ's sake, I beg you, take me away. Have
pity on an unhappy orphan like me; here everyone
knocks me about, and I am fearfully hungry."*
— A.P. CHEKHOV, *Vanka*

1.

A close, humid evening foreshadows rain.
Not night, but dusk, the afterlight of a long day.
Chekhov calls this early darkness a candlelight
tamped down, "a putting out of the eyes."
Chekhov strolls the narrow, rutted road,
peering at the sky
through his pince-nez.
He carries a furled umbrella.

2.

He has moved from his dacha,
four doors down the lane.
Smoke catches his eye,
smoke curling from a chimney stack.
A cottage, modest folk.

> *Oh, how can I get this down*
> *as I go along, see, recall,*
> *everything that's inside that fence?*

3.

The yard of the cottage is
likely a yard for a fieldworker.
Muscle-wrenching. Ploughing. Scything.
A kerosene lamp hangs over a plank table.
Trembling light in the fog.
Is that the family hunched over the table?
Slurping evening tea from their saucers?

4.

A sugar loaf, thick slices, served with tongs.
Black rye bread.
Raspberry jam in a glass jar.
Milk in a red ochre ceramic jug.
Grandmother Chekhov's drinking
glass encased in wire mesh,
almost (but not) filigree.

5.

An older woman, apron wrapped over her
belly under her breasts,
pours from a pot, the tea steaming hot.
On a three-legged wooden stool,
her daughter breast-feeds an infant son.

6.

Playing the hearty host, the father throws
back shots of vodka.
Cucumber pickles, each thick slice crunched,
he mumbles his satisfaction,
and then squints, focuses, a little drunk, on
the cracked ceramic cup
that's been his since he was a boy…
"God will find a way to save me before I die."

7.

The evening is measured in pots of tea.
No conversation, just a slurping satisfaction.
The time chimes.
It's late to bed, it'll be early to rise.
Barefoot yawning children drift off to sleep.
The kerosene lamp's thin flame gutters.
The weary worker, he'll snore
until he wakes himself, snorting, in the morning dark.

8.

Crickets sing,
drunken voices echo off the stars.
A neighbour's dog barks.
On the plank table
a fly crawls half-dead through the dark,
a cat curls under a chair.
Everything is in shadows except for the stars:
intimations of hope.

9.

A sunless morning mist. Increasing drizzle.
Chekhov has forgotten his umbrella.

10.

Olga! Is it raining where you are?
We'll need a chair for me, my wicker chair.

11.

The heavy fragrance of garden flowers.
The cherry orchard in bloom,
almost invisible in the darkness:
What can't be seen may not exist.
Chekhov, so thin, holding a taper, gets up
from his wicker chair.
Taking off his pince-nez, he
examines an unripe cherry.
        My torch. How am I to see?
Across the room, under a crucifix,
a silver-green lampshade
sheds light.
        Can you see? I can hardly see.
        Ah ha! Olga Leonardovna replies. *Ah ha!*

12.

Silence. Only garden insects chirping.
Chekhov's stifled cough.
Olga Leonardovna reclines on a horsehair divan.
She flutters her fan to cool herself.
He refuses to write about his cough,
Or even speak about it.
No future in that.

13.

The third sister, with vehemence,
speaks to the second sister who
questions the first sister, asking:
> *Next year!*
> *In Moscow?*
> *Only. Yes, only.*

Why?

What?

14.

Doctor Chekhov says he will flee
the clear Crimean climate so he can die
consumptive in Germany.

Olga Leonardovna, never cheerful,
always ironical, travels with him by railway carriage.
          Next year? Where did Moscow go?

Tea brewing in the worker's kitchen,
he pours himself vodka
while his wife nurses their youngest son.
He prays the boy will grow up sinewy,
straight, and strong. Good bones!
He casts an eye over the field he ploughs.
It stretches beyond where he can see.
So much work. Too much. For so little.
He feels the lightness,
the relief of an odd little dream: a winter
sun that is always red
though there is no blood.
Grasshoppers
saw their legs, cherries ripen in that sun.

15.

It is done.

THE TWO RICHARDS

PART ONE

"Onegin, my good fellow,
was born on Neva's bank.
A place no different from where you were born…"
     —PUSHKIN, *Yevgeni Onegin*

"A horse, a horse! My kingdom for a horse!"
     —SHAKESPEARE, *Richard III*

I

…the Kazakh steppe, the clickety-clack
of rolling stock…my mother, father,
in one of the several carriages – I am a boy
  going on five…
  heading to the town of Kokchetav.
  We'd boarded at Makinsk,
  closest station to our settlement in the centre
  of nowhere…

exiled from the Leningrad canals –
quartered in a barrack, threadbare
shawls, patchwork coats, footcloths...
    Why this hand-to-mouth life?
    Squatting
    in an oppressive settlement silence –

Now, suddenly, trouble:

    My eye, struck, blood.

Poor boy: child of the remote, desolate steppe.

Weeping, astonished,
what could anyone do?
Tears soaking my bandage, mother's scarf.

    A nurse was called, with her bag of
    pills, needles...

    And then, unexpectedly, for father, all was permitted –

    Take a train on its regional run through Kokchetav!
    The closest hospital on the steppe...

Father & Mother (they'd played
their parts in the Leningrad Theatre...
He'd opened a door with:

A horse, a horse! My kingdom for a horse!

And Mother to me:

Do you hear? Richard. My poor Richard…

My left eye wounded, throbbing,

in pain, sobbing in agony
and she keeps calling…

Richard…?

II

Mother, her Leningrad umbrella held aloft,
genteel for the hour – skip-stepping
puddles…a thin perpetual
drizzle, an outpost station…
the sheen of slick rails running
between nowhere and wherever…
A soldier, lamp in hand:

>   *This is the postal carriage…*

>   *Going to Kokchetav?*

>   *Yes.*

>   *I've got permission!*

A clickety-clack iron horse,
my four-legged ambulance,
the Postal Carriage,
it was the best that could be done,
hunkering down between bulging mail bags…

on the Trunk Line out of Makinsk.

A real dream: canvas bags
of posted letters…gift

boxes...official threats...
old clothes, used clothes, home-made treats,
love in a scrawl...newspaper
news making news.

My eye, searing pain, fingering the bandage
even in my dream
inside sleep, the
scent of Mother's wet scarf,

the sweating soldier staring out into the empty
steppe, holding his lamp...

We lean against the wall to give him room:

Let him pass, always let a soldier pass.

The only chair,
the only chair beside the only window...
There's no window latch. It opens. It shuts.
Soon it will be morning.

Our carriage shakes violently!

The clack of hooves!

Click. Click. Click. We are going faster.
My good eye open, a shroud of darkness

surrounds a bare bulb,
Foucault's swinging Pendulum?
or, maybe a Kazakh church censor?
smoke, sickly sweet…
Sanctus, Sanctus, Sanctus…

A horse! My country…for a bandage!

Saddle me up in my
pain…the throbbing ache,
the turning wheels,
memory whirling
in the storm of
my eye shot through with
the crooked lightning of pain.

III

It was there in a playground behind our barracks…

The neighbour girls:

> Masha, Nadenka, and Inna –
> sifting sand through a toy sieve,
> shuttled from hand to hand…

High-strung Kazakh winds,
shrieking…at play…

Tall swirls of sand.

…girls at play

in their outdoor kitchen…
Two boys with a ball.
I know one of them, Sasha. An older
bully. I shy away from him,
Muscovite. I am Leningrad!
Preferring to play at sifting sand
with girls? Why not?
The girls carry water in a tin can
to make a sand cake.

For you, Vladimir. Cake from Leningrad.

Thank you, Inna.

Masha Nadenka Inna
Inna Nadenka and Masha.
Cooking diligently,
twittering, laughing…
Such nice play, I join in…

> *May I recite a new poem*
> *I recently read?*
> *From this book,*
> The Little Humpbacked Horse,
> *a gift from my mama…?*

We work, you read!

The Little Humpbacked Horse.
> …these brothers having sowed their wheat
> brought loaves of bread…

Vladimir, we love the poem. Pushkin?

Not Pushkin. Pyotr Ershov.

Inna, come home! Inna!

Now there's only two girls
cooking a sand confection…

Cake, Vladimir. Cake!

I made it, too. Mama taught me how to bake.

Don't you know? I'm his wife!

No, never, not on your life.

I am embarrassed:

Two wives are too much for me…
I am too young…

A cloud of sand veers off the Kazakh steppe!
The sky closes on itself, into a yellow fist!

Vladimir? Where'd you go?

Holding my eye! Howling.

Something,
it's like a nail,
it's in my eye!

My nickname, given me by my mother.
RICHARD.
Richie, like the devil, really irritates me.
Richard!

Now is the sandstorm of my discontent.

We're in the train,
wheels, cold steel…

Am I asleep dreaming I'm awake?
The *clack clickety clack*,
a dream beat, a new metallic music –

*Back in the days when my parents were young
there was a craze called – "Concrete music" –*

Musique concrèt…

*No foxtrot, no two-step, no waltzing.
It was the new chic thing, the*
CLACK *of* METALLIC MALEVICH…

His Futurist Opera –
Victory Over the Sun – *Mama adored the Leningrad Theatre.*

And now – for me –
…a rackety clacking carriage,
      a Malevich lullaby…
where pitch dark ends the Kazakh summer,
cold rain zagging across our windowpane…
my good eye open on my poor
Mother shifting in her seat –
a light bulb hanging by a vinyl cord,
a swinging criss-cross of shadows
on the table where a soldier
sleeps, head in his arms, hands linked under his chin…

Snap open – my good eye…

Where's Father? Now?

In his dream…
asleep on the floor
like an old dog's best friend,
on the corrugated floor,
he wakes, strikes a match, squints at his pocket watch:

    Ten-thirty.

    Time has stopped for us, Pavlik…

He rolls onto his side, whispering:

A horse, a horse, my kingdom…

…Never mind…Richard is sleeping.

IV

Cantering through the steppe
…an iron locomotive…
clackety-clack of a waking dream of
pain where I see

HORSES

rearing in Leningrad's disappeared theatre…
a king named Richard…Mother's namesake for me

        the monster

Monarch of England.

But why this stupid name,

bestowed on me in our barracks by my loving mother

who happened to notice one sunny morning that

my right shoulder tilted a little aslant,

the right blade angling up…?

> *Hey! Pavlik!*
> *Our son's right shoulder looks higher than his left!*

A Kazakh X–ray!

What should they do? Could they? What?

SLIGHT CURVATURE of the SPINE…SCOLIOSIS

Tolstoy asked: "What is to be done?"
Chekhov said: "See each thing in its light."

on this deathly silent Kazakh steppe…

She sewed me a shirt, striped poplin, my first fitting…

Where can we find proper medical advice?

Will it heal itself? A special mattress?

Wooden slats laid on top
of my aluminium folding cot.

Who can help?
        Mama of the Workers' Theatre?
        Her career in exile now is…seamstress –
        sewing her fantasies?

Oh, my poor boy. I'll try to stretch your little boy's body.

Give me your hands. No, relax – pull, resist.

Her song has no melody – but still she sings.

> *Oh, my poor son, Prince of Curvature. Order of the Spine. My little hunchbacked Prince, my Richard!*

> *Mama? What kind of stories are loose in your head? your...*

The theatre of Mama's mind excited by Shakespeare! Dreams of great Princes, all the Henrys, Richard, Hamlet on a proletarian stage close by a canal!

V

They – my parents –
had planned to see
Romeo and Juliet

at the theatre on Fontanka…

Romeo's role – announced – yes, the Soviet movie star –
Cherkasov!

> *I said to him, your father: "Buy tickets. Pavlik, show up
> with tickets,"*

Plush chairs, a chance to relax after a day's work.

She couldn't wait to see the beautiful young Romeo,

the great Soviet star Cherkasov –
lithe, muscular, beloved by all Soviet women –
the lights lowered,
the curtain up.

And on stage, there he was, malformed, a hunch of a man,
all aglow in his mal-intent,
Richard III.

Imagine? How could he? Your father bought
the wrong tickets!
Our future aeronautical engineer! Our exiled Hero
of the Soviet Union.
only two things right — Shakespeare and the star,
Cherkasov!
I could barely recognize poor Cherkasov as that
hunched, hobbled monster…
But then, when Cherkasov
let loose a cloudburst of Shakespeare's words:

"Now is the winter of our discontent
Made glorious summer by the sun of York…"

I grabbed your father's hand, shuddered, crying,

Bravo!

And you became my Richard — my Prince…

Mama?

No explanation, no justification:

How come I'm Richard? I was already your Musketeer!

My foolish boy. Our last visit to the theatre
was our goodbye to Leningrad…
Fontanka…Shakespeare…Cherkasov!
Such a marvel…actually seeing him…And then, the
shock…
The delight…

Mama, what I want…is to be a pilot!
Not an aeronautical engineer like father, but a real pilot, in
the air.
I want to fly.

VI

Her love for me was unusual, creative.

She had lady friends who
came by our little room, our little cell, to
drink her carrot tea…

And talk…
talk talk…

Mother's Sunday free time,
her day off, when I was home, too…

A friend –
the one who had the Roman-sounding name –

Agrippina Livovna!

I'd never heard a name like that…

But I liked it – I liked Agrippina
from Leningrad…
not so young,
coming by to gab,
to catch up on the local gossip
with Mother serving tea

…though Agrippina Livovna loved coffee!

Her specialty –
an oak concoction…

coffee of the Kazakh steppe…

acorns with chicory.
Agrippina Livovna slurped two mugs full,
had her first cigarette,
telling Mother this, telling Mother that, this and
that and this…
on a Sunday,
a couple of days
after Kokchetav hospital…
my bandages, post-operation,
removed.

Agrippina Livovna draped
her Kazakh shawl down the back of
our decadent Viennese chair…
where did Mama find that?
and leaning in close to Mother for a
whispered word behind her hand…

(I squat on one of our three-legged milkmaid stools.)

And she rattles on,

Oh, Vladimir, my wounded little boychick –
I forgot your candies – from Nevsky Prospect.
Luba, is it true, only 25 per cent sight left in his eye?
Poor boy.

I'm okay, Agrippina Livovna!
I love caramel!

Oh, my dear boy! I bought you a copy of Murzilka*!*
The children's magazine?
Read me something, go ahead. Aloud. Try.
You know your letters…Ah?

Thank you, Agrippina Livovna!

So many amusing beautifully coloured stories, and the
letters are clear
like a caravan of camels…

I began looking in the book for Camels –
wanting to gather them into words…

Agrippina Livovna!

She downed a second mug
of her acorn coffee…

Tattle prattle…

> *My life, Luba!*
> *Being a journalist in Leningrad…*
> *the last years*
> *I could never write what I wanted,*
> *my last article –*
> *'Children's Education' it was called…about*
> *the great Pestalozzi…*
>
> *In our Workers' Club, yes, yes,*
> *we took courses like his*
> *'Educate Your Future Child'*
> *when my Richard was still inside me,*
> *kicking and fussing.*
> *I even remember some*
> *of his words:*

"Lead your child by the hand into the great vales
of Nature; teach him to go up on the mountain,
to go down into the valley…

"You can drive the devil out of your garden
but you'll find him later among the
bean rows, tended by your own son."

You know, Agrippina Livovna,
think Pestalozzi actually
infected me, inspired me,
gifted me, with my son's love name!

Ah, Luba,
early '30s were
creative –
the Russian avant-garde!
And then!
Almost without warning,
it was all topsy-turvy,
turned inside out

and so here we are in Kazakhstan.

Oh, Agrippina Livovna…
Such poetry…

I want our guest to read *Murzilka* aloud.

Smoke hangs sour in our cell…

My dear friend, Luba,
I remind you – I need to go…
to be gone.

VII

Mother came home from her job,
excited, mysterious…

> *After my shift, I found*
> *on the Security table slotted in*
> *amidst newspapers and brochures*
> *the bright cover*
> *of a child's book. Yes…*
> *for you! I read it back when I was a girl!*
>
> *Were you a girl, Mama?*
> *I thought you were always*
> *Mama…*
>
> *This is no joke, Richard…*
> *This is a book you can love!*

It seems that for sure I have a twin.

> *Mama, the title's so small…*
> *And what's this, these funny horses?*
> *Horses. Horses. Horses…*

My little Prince! Mon pauvre.
This is the poetry of Pyotr Ershov,
so lyrical… The Little
Humpbacked Horse…*!*
Listen again to how this fairy tale begins:

"I tried to neigh, to whinny –

…these brothers having sowed their wheat,
Brought loaves of bread to the royal seat."

In a couple of days, I could recite three
pages of Ershov's *Humpbacked Horse…*

"Let me confess, I am yours to possess.
Find me a cradle and let me rest…"

VIII

Asleep, cradle-rocking in my mother's
lap in our railway carriage that was stacked
corner to corner with postal clutter,
lolling, rocking, rolling from side to side,
the lull of wheels clacking
the stacking of Kazakh correspondence,
the hanging bulb careening…

magic verbs, the steppe, our everyday world beyond words,

one eye blind, one eye open, blurred,

> *A horse, a horse! My kingdom for a camel!*

a pilot, in mid-dream, in mid-
flight, Mother breathing,
Father snoring…
a herd
of circus clowns
beached on canals stampeded by camel horses?
One curvature, one hump, each.

Here I am in midsummer Kazakhstan,
the broad steppe carpeted by blooms,
a cloudless sky…flaring sun, blue moon,
the flaring nostrils of a horse,
a lime-green meadow!

As I lie on the grass,
pain gallops away
on steel wheels, my father is snoring and
I am wearing Leningrad sunglasses.

Why wasn't I wearing these in the sand bakery?
I'd still be able to see, 20 x 20,

      the horses
         cantering…
            circling the Peterhof fountain.

My wounded eye hiding out under Mother's scarf,
and my parents tell me…

   You saw the Peterhof from your baby carriage…

In the waterfall of my dreams
a cataract of mist rising,
I hear my father speaking…

Kazakhstan, harsh, inhospitable –
it is so cold…
while our city by the Baltic Sea
is warmed by the European Gulf Stream…
In midsummer, I dove into the seawater…
Imagine – I once swam out of the lagoon
looking for the Finland Station…

On the train,
the winter wind, when it isn't storming squalls of snow,
is a hard rain…

the Gulf Stream, only a rumour in this land of
hunchback riders.

Don't talk foolish, my father says.

IX

Again, pain!

Our soldier shifts from
cheek to cheek and
turns his head
to catch me crying –

Mother soothing me:

> *Relax, my Richie.*
> *We're almost in Kokchetav…*
> *Lift your right shoulder!*

I close my good eye:

> *Mama, lend the horses your umbrella!*
> *The horses are steaming, dripping wet,*

> *He was shown the Peterhof from his baby carriage…*
> *If he says he didn't see it, then it didn't exist.*
> *What would Pestolozzi say about*
> *any of this, the way I caress the child's*
> *shoulder blade? The slight tilt of the bone?*

I open my good eye – rain..

Rain...rain, run away...

I want to play.
With one of my wives.

X

The rattle
of the train?
The rattle of rain on the windowpane.

The swaying carriage
on the Kazakhstan line to Kokchetav,
a candle in the window,
tilted boxes in transit, bundles, addresses unknown.

Why am I holding Father's hand?
Where is Mother?

Under her umbrella,
sidestepping rain pools,
going tiptoe
into the dank
dark cold
of Kokchetav, so soon?
Though it is still raining softly, there is a full moon.

A shifting shadow of fog,
the voice of my father echoing…

>   *Comrade, sorry,*
>   *the local hospital, is it this way?*

You're coming from the station?
You and your family, lost?
Go back! And
turn left away from the station house,
to the Kokchetav hospital…

The soft drizzle, muzzled rain, a sweet lullaby!

I am in my father's hands!

Vladimir! Open your good eye!
See, here, this room — luminous white!

…frazzled
terrified of the glint of metal,
of a blade's edge,
the night's dazzle.

Mother, talking about her Richard to a doctor!

Father, smoking
Belomor cigarettes
behind the door…

And me, holding chilled air
in my lungs. Listening for the step
of this king
who I know nothing about.
The pale blue sky,
pale white blotting paper,
swollen clouds…

…my kingdom, my kingdom!

Mother, his horse is coming,
pre-dawn riderless ghost
sprinting through
humpbacked clouds…

lovely horse
cantering
ceremoniously
in the king's circus
carousel.

Who are you, O my gracious animal?

Imagining…

a CAMEL
not a horse!

A herd!
Mama's friends:

> *You could collect a caravan,*
> *a caravan of camels from the steppe…*

My eye, my eye, where
has it gone, leaving behind
only pain? I remember the pain.

Nurses and doctors
in angelic white…

> *I'm ready for surgery!*

> *No, no! My Prince,*
> *it's already over,*

> *YOU ARE DONE!*
> *We're on our way home,*
> *back in Makinsk in 15 minutes…*

I smell of antiseptic…
on the sly the pain is gone
for a short stroll.
Father says,
>How droll.
>Even pain
>needs a little air.

I close, open, close, open my healing (so they say) eye –

>*A horse, a camel! My kingdom for a hump!*

Mother laughs and says she's going
to bake me a real cake.

Father asks:
>*What? What?*

He is cross-legged on the floor.
Tired in his bones.

>*What's to become of you, my son? My son.*

The caravan's seven camels
crossing the steppe are
absorbed into the wide-open, unblinking eye
of a red sun.

Johann Heinrich Pestalozzi (1746-1827), Swiss peda-gogue and educational reformer, Romantic in his approach. Because of Pestalozzi, illiteracy in Switzerland was almost eradicated by 1830.

Nikolay Cherkasov (1903-1966), Soviet actor, a People's Artist of the USSR. (He was Luchino Visconti's choice for the lead role of the Prince in *The Leopard* (1963). Because of Cherkasov's health, the producers offered the role to the American actor, Burt Lancaster.)

Kokchetav, now known as Kokshetu, was the administrative center of the Akmola Region in northern Kazakhstan.

Makinsk is the administrative center of the Bulandy District in the Akmola Region of Kazakhstan.

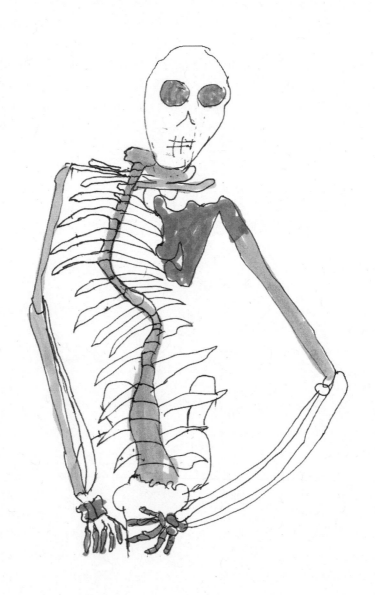

THE TWO RICHARDS

PART TWO

"O, I have passed a miserable night,
So full of fearful dreams, of ugly sights,
That, as I am a Christian faithful man,
I would not spend another such night
Though 'twere to buy a world of happy days —
So full of dismal terror was the time."
                    —SHAKESPEARE, *Richard III*

I

On March 26, 2015,
the maligned King, Richard III,
is unearthed close
to where he was killed
on Bosworth Field when his horse,
White Surrey,
went to its knees and he lost his helmet
and disappeared – after nine blows
to his skull – into the corkscrew
chronicles of Tudor times…
He has had to carry "his curvature story"
like a serpent coiled in his vertebrae bones
from birth, a story
we now know to be a lie.

Half a thousand years of propaganda!

Agnus Dei, qui tollis peccata mundi

By chance,
Richard is risen to light:

> *I come…I come…*

Excavated from under a spray-painted R
(reserved parking) in a car park
that was set for demolition, adjacent to
Greyfriars Church, sanctuary during the Dissolution
of the Monasteries in the District of Leicester…
He, who in my name is risen,
lies in a newly crafted oak coffin carried into
Leicester's Cathedral, a slow-marching procession
to a chant, a trembling organ: Bach, Beethoven…
priests of all orders, nuns
and novices entering into this Feast of
the Astonishing Metamorphosis, Richard,
monster no more, the Shakespearian usurper
is usurped.

The all-out searching, the probing,
the trowel work, the brushing was begun in
September of 2012
at the exact site of his settled bones.
They had been sought and found after a five hundred year
passage under a field, a lawn, an acre of asphalt,
his bone house exhumed,
this notorious rack of vertebrae, the curvature
of his story straightened out, the scientists exultant:

This crooked skeleton belongs to him!

And so:

He's here! Now!

A saga?

Parabolic, unreal…Diabolic?

He, who has *come*, is in my image
in outline,
our twinning begun
by my mother, meaning we are now
inextricably combined,
two of a scoliosis kind.
Me and this King,
Proletarian, divine.

Dressed in a burial suit
bought in a Kenzo Store
on Bruton Street,

made-to-measure
to accommodate the posture

of royal Richard, who – I've been told –
is me as I am him, two in one.
(What fun, no harm done,

as my mother, Luba, might say this
about my little play within this play!)

And so he is borne
out of the ruins of a Franciscan monastery,
out of the grip of mendicant monks,
out of the shallows of shale and stone,
where his skull had lain, slashed open
for want of a horse on Bosworth Field,
finding himself surrounded by Tudor soldiers,
finding his white rose, his white boar, his lineage
stripped of all armour and
carried here to be abandoned
to his own mouldering thoughts,
regal fruit of a crooked plum tree
for five hundred years

My people! I come!
I am done with
Who, in your memory, I'd become.

I was, in fact, a king of good consequence,
deliberate and fair for my time;
I was the king
you cheered in the streets —
not the dark cripple created
by that Stratford versifier…

I remember the wounds to my skull —
I lost my helmet! My white horse,
Surrey, had gone to its knees.
Death cut me down…"
My head left out so the crows
could feed on my eyes and nose…

MUSIC: BACH

II

At the burial pit…the crowd
looks down on me, unaware
that I, child of the Kazakh steppe,
am staring back at them.

Ah, there's Dame Duffy, the mercurial
Laureate. Her poem will be read
At the King's reburial…

Thank you, kind citizens of Leicester…
And who is that young man
smiling so much at our Dame poet?

Don't you remember him?
He's been in lots of films!
*   Cumberbatch! Officially approved,*
he claims he's King Richard's Second Cousin,
16 times removed.

III

Certainly these bones – dusted clean
belong to him – Richard King – as they might, with a
shift of the eye in time, be mine…?
we who share the same hitch in the backbone, more
like a slight swerve in the road (scoliosis)
than a hump in the hills (kyphosis)…

After five hundred years!

Archaeologists feathering a rib, a fibula.

The skeleton seems younger now…

Crouching scholars, after picking at the bones,

are exultant with the DNA and DNK results.

*Eureka! These bones, the head bent to fit the short
hole, are HIM!*

Oh, the mysteries of disease…(Usain Bolt, the fastest
of the fastest men, has scoliosis!)

His noble blood lines are here…!

*(In 2003, as part of a project to identify the possible
remains of Margaret of York – sister of Richard III and
Edward IV – searchers traced an all-female line from
another sister, Anne of York, to a retired journalist in
Canada, Mrs. Joy Ibsen... At the very moment
Richard III's bones were found, his female descendant
died; her son, Michael Ibsen, master craftsman in wood,
travelled to Leicester in her stead)*

    *Being a designer, with my bloodlines bespoke,
    I could create his coffin out of the finest oak.*

(26 March 2015) at Leicester Cathedral.

Inside the church door, *invisible* –
no one sees me make genuflection
at my own resurrection.

*I've only come back to see
if I could compare my
likeness in 3D
to a program with visual
aids, a coloured hologram
that makes the dead man
look like who I am...*

standing in my mind's eye
in the open trench,
I cock my good eye
and peek and see
the right shoulder is me!
Mama Luba would be proud,

I hear her, my beloved mother,
crying aloud: By being yourself
you are another.

And so the same was said, I believe, by
Lady Cecily Neville, Duchess of York:

> *My little Richie! My little hunch, my Prince*
> *you're back. Lift your shoulder! The left. To the right.*
> *Bravo! How hallucinatory!*

This king, if I may say,
having died, lives
to see a better day.

Who said that?

Taxi!

IV

...the Roses had waged War...splayed, spread-eagled

on the bloody meadow, Bosworth Field,

Richard unburied? Perhaps by the River Soar. Or!
Left as carrion.

I was Luba's boy, maybe three years old...
So small...So was he,

taking his royal ease on
an early morning meadow,
Fotheringhay Castle in Northamptonshire...
Rain, the sound of galloping horses...

His hitch-back easily hidden,
Richie, Rick, Dick – so called by his brothers,
who shunned him!
A small boy left alone,
crying!
A gloomy autumn,
October. Even at three,
he was in his saddle
outgrowing his armour, and at last he was
made constable of the county. He was only 18 or 19.

Meanwhile, Mother was
knitting, biding her time.

From inside her womb
I can hear her tears.

So deep inside…

She yelps! Tremors in the walls,
Father – sword in hand
(no jokes please)…Inside in the dark,
eyes shut. Frightening!
In the middle of Mother's contractions,
I hear the midwives whisper:

> It is still early…
> Not a good time to be free…

> No! No! Hurry up please. It's time! Take HIM away!
> Rid me of that child.

My body shakes!
Kicking against
the real and unreal,
an eruption,
a seismic dance
across my body,
Mother in agony, screaming,

her pain mine,
bawling with my mouth closed
preparing to go, through
a break in her waters,
into that outer dark
for a walk
in the park, world without end.

>	*What are you doing to my gentle baby's body?*

Forceps! Shoulder forward, forward into the world…

Sacred voices around Mother's bed:

>	*Pull!*

>	*Harder!*

>	*Yo-oh-heave-ho!*

Am I outside? Where is here?
Eyes shut! I want to see! What in the world is my
future?
To fight on horseback in three battles.
Why 1485?
And where?
Who warms my tiny feet? Who? Is anything
anywhere only because I see it?

Are white tiles the sky I dreamed of
for these nine months!
Upside down? A royal hanging?

Baby Richie! You are arrived in hell!

You will live out your short life,
and after your death – for five hundred long years,

be abused as miscreant and devil! All because of that
toady to the Tudor story, our Bard of Avon.

Hello, my Hell, my life!

Fanfares, deafening!

V

So hard was the birth.

A boy, as the contagion spread,
riding across northern green
meadows flush with bloom –
fragrance of a bastard feudalism...

Fotheringhay Castle.
four brothers, George, a child,
Edward and Edmund,
shapely, tall, almost adult,
close to becoming knights,
the country's rulers,
equal by age and blood...
and then there was the boy –
skinny, bleating, tilted,
leaning into his dream
of his own history...

Rain begins to fall – a yellow mist turning to drizzle,
to pelting, drenching...
Northamptonshire is urgently dark,
chilling, so the brothers put down
their swords...

Are we all here? Thank God! So glad – our horses!

Why are they so nervous?
Stomping, neighing…

To sound an alarm!

> *Horses! Calm down…*
> *It's only rain!*

> *But where's is Richie? Our Prince Richard?*

The boy had bent down to pick a yellow flower…
Then a diabolic cloud, a swirling wind,
lifted his body ….The boy could not run,
could not catch up to his brothers! Lost, alone
with his flower,
he fell into a shallow pool (Solzhenitsyn: "A man
does not drown in an ocean, he drowns in a puddle").

> *Where are you? Richard!*
> *Our future King!*

Oh, my mother! My mind's in a muddle:
Lady Luba, Duchess Neville!
Calling from her carriage, *clickety-*
clack, the rain is non–stop…Father. *Quick to the hospital*!

Sir Geraint – *Quick to the Castle*!
And many small sorrowing birds upon bare twigs
piteously pipe there for pain of the cold
and the boy is in the arms of a white-hatted woman
who sits quietly
sipping acorn coffee…

> *Sorry, so sorry, Lady Cecily,*
> *my Goddess of the steppes –*
> *Lady Luba, so sorry!*

Remember the fragrance
Of yellow flowers on the meadow in the rain…

Where is the grey-beard knight? My father? In exile?

Rattling on about how he dotes on us all.
And me, even more –

> *Richard is my darling!*

Who, so sadly, back against a wall
let a soldier pass and
went out without his coat
into the rain on the meadow of Fotheringhay Castle…

I closed
one eye
and gave Mother
a long careful look…

Goodbye, Sir Geraint!
Cry, cry, there's blood in the rain.
Lift your left shoulder!

I wept like I'd never wept before, though nobody
could hear me howl
except the horses who had iron in their eyes.
And Shakespeare, so cunning, so adept,
he thought I was diabolically funny!

    horse, a horse! My grave for a kingdom!

There was blood in his eye.
The Bard showed no remorse.

I ate my fill of life, its strife.
Like a wanton child-king I took milk wild at the teat
from an antelope…Yes!
And fatted fish from our freshwater rivers.

(Chemical analysis of the teeth and bones of King Richard III
reveals that his diet was decadent even by the standards of
medieval royalty.

During his two-year reign 1483 to 1485, Richard feasted on peacocks, expensive freshwater fish, and other birds, such as swans, cranes, and herons...)

Mama, our whole world is dying...

Eat the drippings of your mama's fish!

Where did your joy run to, my lovely little man?

Mama, you only have to see the play to understand...

VI

Midway through the days of our bard, Sir Geraint,
I was lying in a green meadow
dreaming myself into the scudding clouds,
those schooners with their hidden sailors
flying white and red banners
over our Albion...

Sir Geraint lay beside me on the grass...
the world turned overcast, a leaden grey sky...
an unexpected thunder clash,
the choiring of seven spheres,
the cosmos *gang* awry,
a polyphonic play...
while on a bench under a canvas roof
Sir Geraint made bold to say:

> *I had forgotten in my heart*
> *How to weep, how to suffer pain,*
> *How, through poetry, to impart*
> *In all its rapture, love again.*
>
> *But then – in the wine dark sea*
> *Of ecstasy, I revive...*
> *Tormented, tearful, I thrive,*
> *Words rhyme, come alive in me.*

After that, the *Grene Knyght*, Sir Gawain himself,
living by *cortaysy*, made merry,
dancing carols and joining the entertainments,
desirer libertee
until dark, when a corsair from the steppe
      stopped by to sing a country air:

      Cruel as he may be,
      however quick to kill,
      God can find the way
      to save me, if He will.

      And all who saw him there
      were pleased, and said: I vow,
      never was our king so debonair
      so seemingly without care
      since first he came, as now.[1]

---

[1] Sir Geraint, in his recitation, quoted from both the Gawain
bard and Pushkin.

VII

Leicester Cathedral was crowded,
solemn homage being paid
to Richard the King,
slandered as an icon of evil
in the national vision
for five hundred years.
Economists, chemists, biologists –
and anthro-apologists –
had to accept the revisions implied
in the lie of the bones in his narrow hole.

(CNN) "But while the skeleton's curved vertebrae
are striking, experts say the resulting disability the
King suffered from – idiopathic adolescent onset
scoliosis – would not have been obvious in
Richard III when he was alive. It would have
meant his right shoulder was slightly higher than
the other and so only apparent to the King's closest
family and confidantes."

(CNN) "Portraits of the King, painted some 25 to
30 years after his death, depict him as dark-haired
and steely-eyed; DNA tests strongly argue that he
was blue-eyed and had blond hair."

It was all the big lie! As far as the Bard's eye could see.

Ticket, please, sir. Do you have your ticket?

…I am descended from him…

Right. But you need a ticket?

I hear that the actor,
Cumberbatch…

…He is already
in the cathedral, sir…

Cumberbatch –
is Richard's second cousin 16
times removed.

…That most certainly
may be true.

And my name is also Richard.
I, too, have scoliosis!

None of us are healthy.

Mother, wearing the scarf
that was the bandage
for my eye, whispers: *Oh, Richie.*

At the altar —
our second cousin, Cumberbatch,
has begun to read...

"MY BONES, SCRIPTED IN LIGHT, UPON
COLD SOIL, A HUMAN BRAILLE. MY SKULL,
SCARRED BY A CROWN, EMPTIED OF
HISTORY. DESCRIBE MY SOUL AS INCENSE,
VOTIVE, VANISHING; YOUR OWN THE SAME.
GRANT ME THE CARVING OF MY NAME..."

Oh, my King!

It was in your mind, and it is in mine,
that you and I exist as the
man you are... You did not reinvent but
resumed your dreaming self.
No time to be shy. No one can see us. You've left
the monster behind, dragging himself, the clickety-clack
of the humpbacked bones like a camel across the page:

ENVOI

Richard loves Richard; that is to say,
on this bright sunburst day,
we protest that the play is not the thing:
the myth has died.
I am here for all to see.
I lie down in me,
the best of our past is yet to be.

TORNA A SURRIENTO

AN AFTERLUDE

1.

My compact little condo kitchen.
A small table, stub of
a candle in a candlestick.
Morning pekoe with a Melba biscuit
and the usual Panasonic stereo,
FM 93.6,
bought when I came to Toronto
sixteen years ago.

Sipping tea to the tenor solo of "Torna a Surriento."

> Again and over again
> through all the years.

> A joy,

beginning back home on my Kazakh radio
that hung like a fat saucer, black,
on the whitewashed, warped wall
of our barrack...

2.

The Second World War

News of the Day: *Marshal Zhukov's heroic Red Army
drives General Heinrici's Nazi troops
in retreat out of Poland.*

Then, music:

"The Sugar Plum Fairy," "Pathétique,"
"Sleeping Beauty," "Torna a Surriento."

3.

The New Classical Music. My found
Facebook Friend — Alexa Petrenko.

On this Sunday
    she is my morning lady
presenting Pavarotti

        who sings:

Guarda il mare com'e bello!
Spira tanto sentimento-ohh-ohh-...

Alexa, sending me back
through 93 point 6 to Sorrento...

> Ceramic mug in hand, surviving the war,
> I am so small, the mug so heavy.
> (What is life but big mugs growing lighter
> as the daylight hours grow less interesting?)
> Pavarotti's voice washes over
> the warp in my memory's white wall,
> bread on the table, a wooden spoon, a ladle.
> Then, War interrupts Chaliapin and Shostakovich:

The Red Army streaming into the West in full
battle confidence!

Our national baritone, Yuri Levitan, introduces:

Mikhail Alexandrovich singing
"Back to Sorrento. Come back..."

4.

Am I five? Maybe six?
Eating semolina *kasha* in cotton oil
at the table…Breaking bread –
like the News –
is the sign of our lives
lived: fresh bread, black,
onion rye, sourdough
stale…

5.

The walls of our room closing in
crowded with relatives
we thought dead
in the siege of Leningrad,
all of them fled
from the theatre of war
to our Kazakhstan door.

Alexandrovich ends his song.

My porridge is cold in the bowl.
Holding a spoon of cod liver oil,
Grandmother is fussing at
my shoulder.
I ask:

Where is Sorrento?

Where Alexandrovich is singing?

Yes.

Maybe Italy. Finish your bowl.

But he sang in Russian?

Your mother's late. Eat the drippings, from her fish.

6.

The door opens. Aunt Tanya.
Done with her night shift at the Military Metal Plant.
A girl of 17. Weary.
Grandmother hands her a basin. She washes,
chews on a butt-end of rye torn from a loaf,
hauls a warm mattress down from a shelf above
the brick stove
and lies down to sleep.

Cod liver oil in my mouth,
listening to Aunt Tanya's light breathing,

> I wince like a boy
> drinking vodka for the first time,

and set the oily spoon in the empty bowl.
You'll be healthy as a whale.

7.

Through the window, cold clear almost unbearably
bright skies.

I am shuffling and stacking loose sheets of paper
Aunty has found and gathered
into a heap for her "future artist."
So she calls me, light-heartedly.

A pencil pressed to my lip,
to my tongue, to keep it wet, indelible.
On a sheet torn
from a workbook,
I trace rippled lines,
blue and then
the white caps of the sea.

Baba! The waves of Alexandrovich's Sorrento.

8.

Grandmother is preparing supper,
blood-red beets cut in quarters, blue potatoes,
the eyes plucked.

Somehow I believed
I could draw water
like it was real.
Like it was something I could feel,
an idea I'd begun
to grapple with even
at the age of six.

> *Italia's near the sea?*

> *Don't know, not exactly.*

> *Tanya knows, but she's asleep.*

> *Shh…She's dead tired. Don't wake her.*

Tanya works nights and sleeps days.

Her quiet breathing.

9.

I sit as straight as I can,
eyes closed, and then,
with one eye open I listen,
hoping she will wake
and read from the fat book
she borrowed at the Metal Plant Library,

An American Tragedy.

I know my letters, but I still can't read.
Not sentence by sentence.
Paragraph by paragraph.
I curled myself around an open page
and looked at the letters sideways,
as if the slant of sight might reveal a
special way of seeing.
It did. I didn't know why.
And I still couldn't read.

Tanya's crooning,
the thin girlish voice
of my Aunty
singing a new war song:

> *Wait for me till I come home.*
> *Try to wait for me, and me alone*
> *when you are sad and blue, in pain*

>   *wait, through a pouring yellow rain,*
>   *promise you'll be true…*

She smiles:

>   *I love his songs — our war poet —*
>   *Konstantin Simonov —*
>   *He's married to our Soviet star, Serova —*
>   *the poem is to her.*

She reads aloud from
An American Tragedy.

>   *I prefer tales from the war but*
>   *this tragic story holds my attention*
>   *because Clyde murders Roberta*
>   *while they are boating…*

Myself, I don't like it.

Listening to the radio, I am hearing
about our own everyday tragedies.

Believable? Eventually, everything
becomes believable. There is no end to suffering.

Baba, like a good grandmother, turns down
the suffering on the radio.

10.

Tanya sleeps. Baba whispers:

> *Do you hear Levitan, he sounds so gloomy?*

Tanya sleeps.

> *Our heroic Red Army has won at Kursk!*
> *The greatest tank battle in history, August 25.*

> *I yell hooray.* Tanya is awake!

> *Our army's greatest victory since Stalingrad.*

At the stove, Baba speaks softly.

> *…My two sons were casualties…*

While Tanya slept, I'd gone into our yard.
The bright sun of an August afternoon
was warm but it was windy.
A dust cloud
swirled over the dry yellow grass.

11.

Vladimir!

My friend – a Kazakh girl, Azurihan-Kyzyl,
leaves her house. It's cold but not raining.
She carries a red umbrella.
She's an older schoolgirl, fists
in her cheeks, facing into the coming winter.

Remember how to count in Kazakh?

"Bir"… "eki," "ush," "tort"… "Five?"

… "bes." Repeat – "be-e-es"

I found an empty squirrel's nest. And two more!

What does that mean?
Coming back to our barrack,
high-pitched laughter.

Tanya is stretched out on her mattress.
Beside her, kneeling, are two girls.
A blinding sunset in the window.
They are Tanya's friends.
One is Raya.

12.

Why is Raya wearing a man's cap to cover her fluffy blonde hair?

She turns to me, stops laughing, and says,

Vladimir!

Laughter.
I am lost. What's so funny?
I see that she has a black smear above her lips.
A moustache?
Girls playing at being men, or,
at being grown women with a moustache?
My father has a moustache.

What does a moustache mean?

13.

Baba's sitting at the table because there's no space by the stove,
Near her, a parcel.

Tanya is wearing overalls,
she picks up the parcel. Parcels come, they go,
disappear before my eye.
The girls follow. Disappear before my eye.

Bye, Vladimir.

Tanya kisses my cheek. The slam of the door.
Their laughter vanishes.
People vanish.

Soup is ready.

Baba. I want to draw!

The child endures, despite the war.

I spy...

An indelible pencil. A blue dye.

The Kursk explosions, the stars of war!
In a midnight-blue sky!

14.

Bent over my soup.
Someone new in the doorway.
Too early for Mama Luba.

It's Matthew, young Uncle Matthew.
Usually he sleeps in another barrack.
After working at the Military Plant,
he went back to school.
Grandmother loves him:

My third son,
my only one with a Biblical name!
I have missed you. I see you so rarely…

I lost post-war track of him.
With his beautiful Biblical name…
After that August at Kursk, I lost track…

15.

Forward counting across oceans away. Beside a radio,
in Toronto,
the end of August 2018,
in my compact kitchen,
the small table, a candlestick…

    The phone rings.

My sister calling from Istra, outside Moscow.

    Nina! How are you?
    You okay after the sanatorium?

    This August is not too hot. I walk a lot. But I am
    Calling – my brother – to give you the phone number
    of our Uncle Matthew.

    Matthew…?

    He is 93 today!

    Uncle Matthew, 93?

    I promised him your greetings.

       CLICK

Happy birthday, Uncle Matthew! This is Vladimir.

*Vladimir? Nephew? Your boy's voice is still
in your voice…*

That's me, Uncle. Still dreaming of the sea.

You became an architect?

I was. Retired now.

Your drawings are in all my notebooks!

You've got your notebooks to hold on to.

*During your childhood, we were never close,
what with my job…*

Tanya read me your books. I loved my Aunty.

She was my last loss…She died two years ago…

16.

Music. In my kitchen.

Naples calling at 96 point 3
on my Panasonic stereo –
bought 16 years ago,
        long after, at my aunt's knee
        I heard the same call
over a round black radio
hanging on a
warped Kazakh wall.

Alexa Petrenko speaks memory:

    Luciano Pavarotti… "Come back to Sorrento,"

a town somewhere in Italy near the sea
where the sky's often the exploding blue
envisioned by a child
sitting up straight with one eye open in the early darkness,
a child with a pencil…

Vladimir Azarov is an architect and poet, formerly from Moscow, who lives in Toronto. He has published: *On the Death of Ivan Ilyich; Three Books; Of Architecture* (with illustrations by Nina Bunjevac); *Seven Lives; Sochi Delerium; Broken Pastries; Mongolian Études; Night Out; Dinner With Catherine the Great; Imitation; Of Life and Other Small Sacrifices; The Kiss from Mary Pickford: Cinematic Poems*; and *Voices in Dialogue: Dramatic Poems* – and with Barry Callaghan, *Strong Words,* translations in an English/Russian bilingual edition, of Alexander Pushkin, Anna Akhmatova, Andrei Voznesensky (into a second printing).